THE MISSING POM MYSTERY

CURLY BAY ANIMAL RESCUE COZY MYSTERY BOOK 1

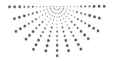

DONNA DOYLE

Publisher's Note: This is a work of fiction. Names, characters, places, and incidents are a product of the author's imagination. Locales and public names are sometimes used for atmospheric purposes. Any resemblance to actual people, living or dead, or to businesses, companies, events, institutions, or locales is completely coincidental.

© 2021 PUREREAD LTD

PUREREAD.COM

CONTENTS

Chapter 1	1
Chapter 2	11
Chapter 3	20
Chapter 4	32
Chapter 5	41
Chapter 6	51
Chapter 7	59
Chapter 8	75
Chapter 9	86
Chapter 10	99
Other books in this series	107
Our Gift To You	109

CHAPTER ONE

Courtney Cain slammed the empty cardboard box on her desk, even though it did very little to diffuse the anger she felt swelling inside her chest. After the last ten years, after all she'd done for Miller and Martinez Marketing, they'd let her go with little more than a memo on a crisp sheet of paper. The president hadn't even bothered to sign it himself, but he had his secretary use a stamp instead. She slammed this on the desk next to the cardboard box as she began packing up.

"Whoa, are you okay?" Lynn, her dark blonde hair perfectly coifed above the collar of her dark power suit, stopped as she strode by on her way to the copy room.

Courtney clunked her coffee mug into the box with a bang, followed by numerous other random objects from her desk. She wasn't even entirely certain as to whether or not they were hers or the company's, but she could hardly see for the tears in her eyes. "Oh, I'm fine. I'm perfectly fine. Everything is just peachy. Just like always."

Lynn put two and two together as she watched Courtney pack her things. "Did you get fired?" she whispered. "But that's impossible! You're so good! You're the one who created that fantastic ad for the Smithton car dealership. They couldn't possibly let you go!"

"Just let it be a warning to you never to let your guard down around here. The place is full of snakes." Courtney sniffled as she yanked open a desk drawer and began emptying it as well.

"Oh, honey. I'm so sorry." Lynn scratched the side of her neck. "So, um, I suppose this means you won't be needing that new ergonomic chair anymore, hmm?"

Snapping her head up and feeling like the evil, misunderstood witch in a fairytale, Courtney smacked her hands on the desk and growled. "Get out."

"Right." Lynn skittered out of her office and down the hall, no doubt to spread the word to anyone who hadn't managed to already catch it through the grapevine.

Panic was swimming up underneath Courtney's anger. This had been the best job she could've stumbled into when she was fresh out of college and looking for some direction in her life. She'd started out low on the totem pole, but that had been expected, and Miller and Martinez Marketing was wonderful about promoting from the inside. Once Sam Smythe had taken notice of her for more than just her marketing skills, she'd thought the sky was the limit. Everything was perfect. Everything was falling into place. She couldn't possibly ask for more.

Now, she was free falling back down to the ground after being so unexpectedly pushed off this mountain she'd built. Courtney had never expected this news when she'd stepped into her manager's office. She'd land lower than where she'd started from, considering getting fired was going to be a massive black mark on her resume. Nobody would hire her now. She'd never get back into marketing, and it didn't matter how good she was at it. She didn't know what she was going to do.

"Hey, Court. Just thought I'd come by and check on you. I, uh, I heard you weren't taking the news well."

She lifted her eyes to find Sam Smythe standing in the doorway of her office. Just a day ago, had she been going through some tragedy, she would've welcomed his presence with open arms. Now, not so much. "What do you want?" she snapped.

"Hey, now," he said smoothly, pulling aside his suit jacket so he could stick his hands in his pockets. "Everything is going to be all right. There's no need to get angry or cause a scene."

Courtney scowled at him, holding his gaze as she raked her hand across the stack of papers on the corner of her desk that held the carefully plotted marketing scheme for one of the firm's biggest clients. The sheets went whirling into the air. "I haven't even started to make a scene yet!"

His eyebrows drew together, and his jaw clenched as the papers hit the floor and the bookcase one by one. This was just the type of disorder that Sam couldn't stand. "This isn't necessary, Courtney. These decisions are simply business. You can't take it so personally."

"No?" she questioned, coming around the desk toward him. "You personally voted to have me sacked. You sat up there in that board room and said you wanted me gone!"

"It's not like I was the only one!"

"Yeah. That helps." The one thing it did help with was bringing back her anger instead of that panic she'd been working on. The anger was easier. "Just get out of here, Sam. Just leave me alone while I pack up the last decade of my life into this little box."

"All right. I get that you want some time alone. That's perfectly normal. You take a little time, get your things, go home, and relax. I'll pick you up for dinner around eight. We'll do something special, like Chez Sophia." Sam smiled at her, waiting for her to gush about what a wonderful idea he had.

Instead, she just stared at him. At one point, Courtney had thought he was one of the most handsome men in the world, with his perfect hair and lantern jaw. Now, she noticed he was really just trying too hard with his designer suit, expensive loafers, and weekends at the health spa. Even worse, he always thought he was right. He never apologized, even when he was in the wrong. He simply waited for others to tire of being angry with him. Well, that wouldn't happen again.

"You know what?" she said, forcing a smile onto her face. "I'll get my things. And I'll go home. And I'll even try to relax and forget about this whole horrible day. But if your smug face shows up on my doorstep, I'll punch it right in!"

Sam took a step back, shocked. "Courtney! You don't mean that! You're not a violent person. You're just letting all this get to you."

"As it should!" Courtney marched up to him and poked him in the chest with her finger. "You think you're so wonderful and so talented, but you're just a big phony like all the rest of the suits who sit in that board room. I don't ever want to see you again, Sam Smythe! Not today, or any other day!"

He let out a breathy laugh as he smoothed down his shirt. "You don't mean that. No woman has ever broken up with me before."

"And I've never been fired before, but I suppose there's a first for everything! Now get out!"

Much to her relief, Sam strode off down the hall. He would no doubt keep their conversation private, not because he didn't want to embarrass her, but because he wouldn't want anyone to think *she'd* actually been the one to break up with *him.*

Taking one last look around her office, Courtney headed for the elevator. She'd grown so used to working here. All the little noises, from the ding of the elevator to the murmur of voices in the breakroom, had become the background music for her day. She knew the maze of offices like the back of her hand. She had her commute timed down to the minute, even accounting for different kinds of weather. Miller and Martinez Marketing was ingrained in her, and she had no idea how she was going to pick herself up and move on.

Putting the box in the backseat of her car, she grabbed her headset and called the one person she'd always been able to count on no matter what happened in her life. "Hey, Mom."

"What's wrong, sweetie?"

Courtney smiled. Her mother always knew, even before she'd said anything. "I just got fired." Saying it out loud to her mom made all the panic overflow into tears. "Mr. Woodson called me into his office, and I thought he wanted to go over some of the accounts I was working on, but he informed me the board had decided to let me go!" She laid her forehead on her steering wheel and let out a sob.

The sound of pots and pans in the background hit her ears. Mrs. Cain was always busy in some form or fashion. If she was up, she was cooking, cleaning, or gardening. If she was sitting down, she was cross-stitching or knitting. "Oh, honey. I'm so sorry."

"And to make it worse, Sam helped them kick me out! I broke up with him, and now my whole life is ruined!"

Mrs. Cain let out a grunt. "Darling, you know I love you, and that's exactly why I'm going to tell you not to think that way. You can be angry. You can be frustrated. You can even cry. But you absolutely can't go around thinking your life is over."

"But—"

"No, no. God never lets anything happen without a reason, even if we're not able to understand it at the moment. If you've lost your job, then you're probably better off without it. They always did want you to work long hours, and you had to go in on the weekends far too much. As for that Sam Smythe, well, I don't have anything nice to say about him and so I won't. But you're better off without him, too."

"Yeah. Maybe." She knew her mother was right, at least about Sam. Courtney had fallen for his song and dance routine, but he'd already revealed his true side to her. It would likely be harder to get over her lost job than her broken engagement, and that certainly said something about her relationship. Courtney started the car and pulled out into traffic as she mopped her tears off her cheeks. "So, what do I do now?"

"Everyone has their own way of dealing with these things. Just don't take too long to grieve for what you've lost before you start figuring out what new opportunities are out there waiting for you."

Courtney smiled through her tears. "Thanks, Mom. You're the best."

"So are you, sweetie."

Her apartment was far too quiet when she got home and plunked the cardboard box down by the front door. She would go through it later. After eating some leftover lasagna, Courtney decided there was no point in waiting. She could take action right now.

A quick internet search turned up plenty of jobs like the one she'd just had. There were many positions right there in the city for account executives and marketing pros. It was all about sales, and she was good at that, but her heart called out for something different. She widened her search parameters.

"Curly Bay Pet Hotel and Rescue," she read, surprised to find anything that had to do with animals. "Seeking a new manager for prestigious pet day spa and community-centered rescue. Must be good with people and pets and have excellent managerial skills. Will manage all aspects of the business, including community outreach and marketing."

Courtney smiled. Curly Bay was over an hour away near the coast. It was a tiny little town, and completely different than everything she was used to. She immediately sent in her resume.

CHAPTER TWO

Two weeks later, Courtney pulled up in front of the Curly Bay Pet Hotel and Rescue. It was a long, plain building, and she'd seen the kennels that flanked each side of it as she'd driven up. The large sign in the center above the entrance doors proclaimed she was in the right place, and she tried to remind herself that it was true. Not that she doubted the location on her GPS, but whether or not a woman like her, who'd been wearing suits and attending numerous meetings, was really the right person for this job.

"Don't sweat it," she said to her reflection as she adjusted the collar of the dark blue polo she'd put on, along with a pair of khakis. "You've got this. Besides, you've already rented a new place and moved all the way down here, so there's no backing out now."

The lobby had a long counter that ran across it and seating on either side to accommodate each aspect of the place. Courtney stepped up uncertainly. "Hi. I'm looking for Ms. O'Donnell. I'm Courtney Cain."

The older woman who'd been frowning at a computer now looked up and frowned at her. She had gray hair cropped close to her head and oversized glasses that didn't exactly do her any favors. "The new manager. Right. Just a sec." She disappeared through a door behind the counter.

A new woman showed up a moment later and immediately ushered Courtney around behind the counter. "Miss Cain! It's so nice to finally meet you in person. I'm Ms. O'Donnell, of course. You met Dora, and that's Jessi over there." She waved at a younger woman who was on the phone. Jessi fluttered her fingers in a wave. "I'll give you a full tour of the place and then you can get started."

"All right." Courtney had expected to fill out employment and tax forms, but she wasn't going to argue.

"Let's start over here." Ms. O'Donnell led the way to the rescue side, her blonde hair bouncing around her shoulders. The place was already a maze, since this door led to yet more doors. "We have an area for cats and another for dogs, keeping them as separate as possible. Occasionally, we get in a rabbit or a potbellied pig, or even a few birds. We make special accommodations for them. Let's explore the dogs, first."

Courtney's ears were accosted with sound as soon as Ms. O'Donnell opened the door to the kennels. The pups sensed that there were humans nearby, and they immediately came to the fronts of their cages for attention.

Ms. O'Donnell paused at each kennel, putting her hands through the chain link to love on each dog. "I started this place out as just a rescue when I found a stray dog. I didn't want to take him to the pound and risk being put down, but I couldn't have him at my apartment, either. I won't bore you with all the details, but soon enough I had myself a pet rescue. Unfortunately, it's awfully expensive to run. That's when the hotel and spa started, strictly as a way to fund this side of things."

Courtney reached in to ruffle the ears of a little terrier. She'd always loved animals growing up, but it'd been so long since she'd had one of her own. "I don't know how you manage not to bring them all home with you."

Ms. O'Donnell's thin lips parted in a smile. "It's not easy, but I do enjoy the time that I spend here with them. Plus, seeing them go to a good home makes all the difference." She brought Courtney to a chart on the wall. "We have all the detailed information on the animals in the computer, but right here we keep track of when they were fed, bathed, walked, and brushed. Jessi does most of the work on this side, but she'll need as much help as possible since there are so many animals. All the leashes are right here on this rack, and the dogs each have a little run outside they can access at any time. If you want to take them for an actual walk, you just go out the back door there."

"That sounds simple enough." Courtney's uncertainty was quickly lifting. She would be busy, but she didn't mind, and this kind of work would definitely be satisfying. Instead of appeasing corporate executives with her ad ideas, she'd truly be helping someone in need.

"The cats are a similar story," Ms. O'Donnell explained, bringing Courtney into the cat room. The felines meowed at her through the bars of nice little apartments stacked up on each side of the long room. The chart for their feedings and litter box cleanings was on the back of the door, and a play area had been set up at the end of the room for potential adopters to visit with the animals.

Courtney scratched a white cat's back, already in love. She had wasted so much time working in an office!

"Let's tour the hotel, shall we?"

Courtney held back a gasp at the luxury of this end of the building. Everything on the rescue side had been perfectly clean and serviceable, if a little battered here and there. But it was clear there wasn't room for anything less than the absolute high end when it came to the hotel. It was similarly arranged to the rescue side, except that the kennels and cages were more spaced out and private. She noticed there was also a big difference when it came to the kind of animals here. While there were mutts galore in the rescue, every animal here looked like it had probably won a ribbon in a show somewhere.

"Now, the hotel and spa are incredibly important to this business. People pay a ridiculous amount of money to know their pets are perfectly pampered. We don't have a wall chart here because it would be too hard to keep track of everything that each pet needs. You'll find a file folder next to each cage, instead. Some of them are simply here for grooming or a nail trim, and others are here to stay with us. It might just be for the day while their owners are at work, or it could be for a week while their owners are on vacation. They each have their own bins of food, which are never to be mixed up, especially since most of them are on strict diets."

"Wow," Courtney breathed as she picked up the chart for a Maine Coon who sat grumpily at the back of his cage and glared at her. He had a long list of needs that were to be met every day, including being groomed with a special brush twice daily. "These are some pretty pampered pets."

"Absolutely," Ms. O'Donnell confirmed. "They belong to the most prestigious people in the area, and their owners expect nothing but the absolute best. Both the owners and the pets should be treated like royalty. That's what keeps them coming back, you know."

Courtney made a face as she realized some of those people were probably just like Sam Smythe, on the top of the corporate ladder and looking down at everyone else. Great.

"Dora takes care of almost everything on this side. She does all the grooming and nail clipping and whatnot, but she may need some assistance with walking or cleaning out cages. Otherwise, just let her do her thing. She's the best groomer in all of Curly Bay."

"Can do." Courtney knew the basics of brushing or trimming nails, but she wouldn't want to attempt the fancy haircut she spotted on a nearby poodle.

"Security is also of utmost importance. We're talking about animals who're not only pedigreed, but prize winners as well. It's incredibly important that there's never even a chance for them to get out. The back door here should be locked at all times." Ms. O'Donnell pointed to the bolt on the inside of the door. "There's a security camera out back, but something happened with the wiring and it doesn't work. It's just for show until we get it fixed."

"I understand." Courtney nodded, wanting to make sure she absorbed everything. This was a brand-new job, and there was no room for mistakes.

"Here in the center of the building is the office." Ms. O'Donnell led the way back into the reception area and through the door she'd first come out of. They were in an open office area cluttered with several desks, numerous filing cabinets, and a coffee station. Another room off the back served as a supply closet for pet food and cat litter. Ms. O'Donnell pointed to the one desk in the room that wasn't already covered in papers and files. "Your desk is right here."

It certainly wasn't the executive office she was used to. Courtney would be working right in here among everyone else instead of in a private area with her name on the door. The desk was old and battered, and she highly doubted the wooden drawers had ball bearing slides. There wasn't even a window where she could sip her coffee and overlook the cityscape. She smiled. It was completely different, and that made it perfect.

Ms. O'Donnell put her hands together with a clap. "Well, I think that about does it! I'm going to head off to run a few errands, and I'll leave you to it."

"Don't you want to train me on the paperwork or how to do intakes?" Courtney had done her best to brush up on what it was like to work in the animal industry. The internet and some magazines had been some help, but that didn't mean she knew all the nuances of this particular business.

The owner waved her hand in the air nonchalantly. "Everything is fairly well all laid out. The paperwork is organized into binders up at the reception desk, and Jessi and Dora will help you as well."

"Right. Um, do you mind if I ask what happened to the previous manager?" That was something that'd been on her mind quite a bit since she'd applied for this job, wondering what would make someone leave it if it sounded so great.

"Oh." Ms. O'Donnell lifted her shoulders in a dismissive shrug. "She got some fancy job in the city."

"I see."

"Have a wonderful day, and I'll see you tomorrow morning!" Ms. O'Donnell left.

Courtney tried to squash down the choking feeling in her throat. She was excited about this job, and she was more than happy to do it, but the fact remained that she didn't really know *what* her job consisted of. Ms. O'Donnell had only told her that Jessi would need help on the rescue side and Dora would run most of the work on the hotel side. She didn't really know what her daily routine should consist of or what, exactly, she should be managing. "Great," she whispered to herself as she ran her finger along the shabby edge of her desk. "Just great."

CHAPTER THREE

An hour later, Courtney was up at the front desk. She'd answered the phone numerous times, but she always had to either pass the call off to one of the other staffers or put the call on hold until she could figure out the answer to the question. Now, she was trying to run a payment for someone picking up their pet after a grooming session.

"I'm sorry. This is my first day and I'm still learning the ropes," she said as she poked her head around the corner into the office. "Jessi, could you help me out? I'm not sure how to do this."

With a little sigh, Jessi got up from her desk and came out to the reception area, clicking away on the computer. "Just pull the dog up by the owner's name here, in this program. It'll calculate the amount for you automatically as soon as you click here to show the pet is getting picked up. Then you can swipe the card through the machine like this."

Courtney tried to give her utmost attention to Jessi's instructions. It was all fairly straightforward once she knew how to do it, but she'd needed someone to at least point her in the right direction. "Thanks," she muttered when Jessi was done, and the customer was on his way out the door with a perfumed pug. "I'm sorry to disturb you on your lunch."

"It's okay. I mean, Ms. O'Donnell didn't exactly do you any favors. That's just how she's always run the place, though. She has very good intentions, but she doesn't know much about business."

That explained a lot, potentially including why the previous manager had left. "I'll get the hang of it all soon."

"I know you will," Jessi said with a smile. "When the front desk dies down this afternoon, I could use your help getting all the dogs walked."

"Can do." That, at least, was something that didn't require any technical experience beyond clipping a leash to a collar.

The next customer through the door was clearly coming in for hotel and spa services. She was dressed in a bright pink dress with a wide vee neckline that showed off the years she'd spent in the sun. The large black belt held back her stomach and matched the expensive looking heels she tapped in on. The Pomeranian she held under her arm was dressed to the nines as well, sporting a little green polo. His fur exploded out from the sleeves and hem.

"Hello! How can I help you?" Courtney asked, poised to be as professional as possible even though she had no idea what she was doing.

The woman frowned deeply. "I'm here to drop off Sir Glitter for his doggie daycare, of course. Isn't that right, my little snookums? Aren't you here to have some time at the spa while mummy does her running? Yes, that's my little sweetness." She said this while making kissy faces at her dog, who mostly ignored her.

"Of course. And what's your name, please?" Courtney held her fingers at the ready over the keyboard, hoping she could get this done without irritating this woman any more than she already had.

The customer let out an annoyed sigh. "Mrs. Throgmorton. Really. I've been coming here for a long time, and I can't imagine that anyone wouldn't know."

"It's my first day, but I'm sure we'll get to know each other just fine." Courtney typed the last name into the system, glad she didn't find multiple entries. She could only imagine the hissy fit the woman would throw if Courtney dared ask for her first name. Fortunately, there was only Mr. and Mrs. Throgmorton and their one pet, Sir Glitter.

"Let's hope so. Sir Glitter gets nothing but the absolute best of everything. I wouldn't dream of dropping him off at just any old kennel, you know." Her deep, husky voice instantly changed into the higher pitched one she used for her dog as she once again pressed her face against his fur. "That's right, because my sweet little Glitter-Witter deserves it, doesn't he? Yes, he does! He's just the best boy! Yes, he is!"

"All right, I've got him in the system, so I can take him for you." She'd done enough intakes already this morning to know that regular daycare customers who were already in the system didn't need any additional paperwork. Yet another miracle.

But as she reached out for the puffy Pomeranian, Mrs. Throgmorton held him tighter to her chest. "Hold on. First, I'd like to know that he'll be getting his regular kennel. He doesn't like change, you know, and I won't have him stressed out by being on the wrong side of the room."

Oh, yes. Heaven forbid the poor dog not have his requested kennel. Courtney could tell it was going to be much more frustrating to deal with the hotel customers than any other duties here. "I do see a note here in the system that indicates which kennel he likes, so his reservation is all set."

Still Mrs. Throgmorton held him tightly. "Do you also have a note for Dora about giving him a trim? Now that the weather is warmer, I'd like his hair to be a little shorter so he won't get too hot when we're at the pool together."

Biting her tongue against asking if Sir Glitter had his own set of swim trunks, and probably not wanting to know the answer, Courtney smiled. "Yes, it seems that everything is in order."

"Well, all right." Mrs. Throgmorton finally surrendered the pup over the counter. She touched the tip of his nose with her finger. "Mommy will be back this afternoon, my little cherub. You be a good little boy, and we'll go out for a treat. Who's the most handsome little baby? Who is it? Who is it?"

Sir Glitter let out an ear-shattering yap that must've served as the appropriate answer, considering the resulting grin on Mrs. Throgmorton's face.

"What time should we expect you back?" Courtney asked.

"Six. As usual." She added this last phrase with a bit of hostility, but at least she turned around and left.

After installing Sir Glitter in the requested kennel and making sure Dora knew he was there, Courtney had an overwhelming few hours at the reception desk. A man from Animal Control showed up to drop off a beagle that he'd been informed would go to the Curly Bay Rescue's adoption program. Another customer came in who'd already adopted from the rescue but needed to return the dog due to it not getting along with her cat. Then there was a customer whose credit card wouldn't run through the machine. Instead of simply giving her a different card, he insisted on calling his bank and running through every single transaction.

Courtney was still dealing with the supposed bank error when an older gentleman entered in a slim suit that didn't really go with his cowboy hat and boots. He gave Courtney a friendly smile as he stepped up to the counter and touched the brim of his hat. "Hi, there! I'm Mr. Throgmorton. My wife brought in her dog earlier."

"Oh, yes. Of course. I'm sorry. I didn't think anyone would be here for him until six." Courtney checked her watch just to be sure, but the hours were indeed dragging by just as she thought they were.

"No, no. I'm just here because my wife forgot to give him his treat today. You know how she is about that dog, and I thought I'd bring it by."

However nasty Mrs. Throgmorton had been, her husband was much kinder. It was a big relief to Courtney. "Sure. I'm kind of busy at the moment, but if you leave it with me, I can get it to him."

"I can just run back and do it really quick, and save you some time."

"That would be fine." She smiled and waved him back behind the counter just as the man with the bad debit card walked back up.

"Thanks. That dog means the world to my wife, and heaven help us all if anything were to happen to him." He held up the treat intended for Sir Glitter as he headed for the kennels.

"I've discussed the matter with the bank, and they seem to have found the mistake. Unfortunately, it's going to take them some to correct. A computer error on their part, I'm told. In the meantime, I'll just give you my credit card. Understand, though, that this isn't my fault. There's plenty of money in there."

Courtney certainly hoped so, since he was trying to pay for very expensive services that certainly couldn't be considered essential by most people. It wouldn't make sense for anyone to waste their money on the pet spa unless they had plenty of it to go around. She reminded herself that his budgeting matters weren't her concern. "Not a problem. I'll get everything squared away."

"Thanks again!" Mr. Throgmorton called with another touch to his hat brim as he strode back through the lobby. "Have a good afternoon!"

"You, too!" At least one customer had been pleasant.

The next one was simply odd. Though his head was shaved completely bald, he had a very thick and curly mustache that instantly reminded Courtney of a Labradoodle. She tried not to stare at it as he strode up to the counter. The mustache tipped up at each edge, indicating he was smiling.

"What can I do for you today?" Courtney asked politely.

"I'd like to adopt a dog."

Her returning smile was genuine. Though she hadn't had the time for a pet while working at Miller and Martinez Marketing, Courtney always wanted to help an animal in need. For the last ten years, she'd simply been donating to the shelters whenever she'd had a little extra cash. Now she was getting to be part of the process firsthand, and her heart lifted in her chest as she imagined him finding the perfect dog to take home. "That's wonderful! I can take you back and let you meet some of them."

"Actually, no." He waved his hand through the air to stop her. "There's a certain kind of dog I'm looking for. I'd like a Pomeranian."

"Oh, I see." She quickly scanned through the pictures and in the computer system. "We have several small mixes, but nothing purebred."

"Nothing at all?" he pressed.

"No. The only Pom in the place is one who's staying in the hotel, and of course he already has an owner. But if there's a certain quality you're looking for in a dog, then I'm sure I can help you." Or rather, Jessi could help him, since Courtney didn't yet know the dogs' personalities.

The man's brow wrinkled as he scratched a hand through that curly mustache, and he gritted his teeth together in frustration. "The only quality I'm looking for is that it be a Pomeranian. I'm not going to bring home just any old mutt."

Courtney felt insulted for all those mutts that were back there waiting for homes. It wasn't their fault they didn't have all the 'proper' breeding. "Then I'm afraid I can't help you today. Perhaps I could take your name and number down, and if we get one in, I can give you a call." She wasn't sure if that was even anything the Curly Bay Pet Hotel and Rescue normally did, but it seemed like a good way to provide customer service, even though she couldn't truly help the man.

"Why don't you just let me see the one you have in the hotel?" he asked, leaning over the counter and craning his neck toward the hotel door. "Perhaps the owner would be willing to sell it to me."

"I think not." Courtney didn't know the Throgmortons well, but it was clear they wouldn't part with their pooch.

"You never know until you ask," he insisted. "Just let me see. I'd really like one of the cream ones, although an orange would be all right, I suppose."

Courtney cleared her throat. Sir Glitter was a beautiful cream color. "I'm sorry, but I can't let you back there."

"Just a peek! Or you could give me the name of his owner?"

Courtney hadn't imagined having to deal with a security issue here at all, but it was even more disturbing that it was happening. "We guard the privacy of our hotel guests very carefully, and I'm going to have to ask you to leave now." She pointed toward the door to drive her statement home.

The mustached man huffed. "Fine, but you'll be hearing about this. I'm sure everyone on the internet would be more than happy to see the terrible review I'll leave for this awful place!" He slammed his fist down on the counter before turning to leave.

As the workday wore on, Courtney truly began to wonder if she'd made a mistake. There was so much work to do at the front counter that she hadn't even had a chance to check on Dora or Jessi unless she was harassing them to help her. She hadn't even made it through a full day yet, and she was already starting to wonder if she'd made the right decision by taking this job.

CHAPTER FOUR

"Courtney! We've got a problem!"

Courtney had been frowning at the computer screen. The steady influx of customers they'd seen throughout the day had finally waned, and she'd taken the time to familiarize herself with the various programs. Or at least, she was trying to. It all seemed very disorganized.

She turned to see Jessi at her shoulder, a worried look on her young face. "Sir Glitter is missing!"

"What?" Courtney's heart fell into her feet. All the animals here were important, but she knew what a big deal Sir Glitter was. "Are you sure?"

Jessi grabbed Courtney by the arm and dragged her back to the hotel side, gesturing wildly at the empty cage that'd held the little puffball earlier in the day. "I came over here to see if Dora needed any help. I noticed the door was open, and I assumed she had him in the grooming room. But she didn't."

"Nope," Dora affirmed with that permanent frown she'd been wearing all day. She had her arms folded over the front of her pink grooming apron. She gestured over her shoulder to the door that led to the grooming room. "I was finishing up on a Yorkie."

"Okay. He has to be around here somewhere. He couldn't have just disappeared." Courtney was trying to stay calm, but she was panicking on the inside. It was her very first day managing this place, and already a dog had gone missing! "When was the last time someone had him out?"

"We haven't," Dora said with a glare. "Several of the dogs have been late for their potty breaks today, since we're running short staffed."

"Don't be like that," Jessi hissed under her breath.

But the words had already been spoken, and Courtney knew Dora meant her. "I'm doing my best to keep up with things but considering how much is going on around here we should have more than three people trying to keep track of it all. Now, whether he was late for a potty break or not really isn't important. It's a matter of when his cage door was opened last. Did anybody take him out of his cage so far today?"

Both women shook their heads.

"All right. And I didn't, either. That means either I didn't do the latch on his kennel properly when I put him inside, or he's a smart little thing and he opened it himself. Let's just look around. He couldn't have gotten far." The dog was small, and there were plenty of places for him to hide. The three women started looking around the hotel, checking behind doors and around all the furniture. Sir Glitter didn't turn up.

Nor had he wandered into the office or storage room, where Courtney was very much hoping they'd find him with his little face stuffed into a bag of cheap kibble meant for the rescues. When he wasn't there, they checked the rescue side, still to no avail.

"I just don't understand," Courtney said when they returned to the hotel. "He's not magic. He can't just disappear. Even if he managed to get out of the kennel itself, he'd have to get out of the building. I'd see him if he went out the front door, and the back door is latched." She reached out to yank on the handle to prove it.

But the back door swung wide open.

"Now you've done it," Dora remarked.

Courtney felt like she was walking through a nightmare. She shut the door again, then reopened it. "I didn't use this door, and I saw for a fact that it was latched this morning!"

"The most important thing right now is to find the dog," Jessi reminded them. "Dora, you've still got grooming appointments to get done, so you can stay here and mind the phones. Courtney and I will go outside to look." She jetted out the back.

Courtney followed, wishing she'd been the one to create the plan. It'd be nice if she could at least sound as though she knew what she was doing. Jessi had worked here longer and knew the business better, but that didn't do anything to soothe her ego.

"Sir Glitter!"

"Come here, boy!"

"I've got a treat for you!"

There was a small field behind the Curly Bay Pet Hotel and Rescue, and this served as a place to take the dogs for walks. With only a few trees and a privacy fence on one side that delineated the property line, they covered the area quickly without finding any sign of the little dog.

"This isn't good," Jessi said when they reconvened by the back door. "We've got to call Ms. O'Donnell."

"I'll get her on the phone if you can contact animal control. They need to be on the lookout for Sir Glitter, as well." Courtney put in a call to her new boss, not surprised nor pleased when Ms. O'Donnell told her to call the Throgmortons as well.

She cleared her throat as she listened to the other end of the line ring, hoping they wouldn't answer and she'd find Sir Glitter before anything actually came of this. She'd been fired from her job in the city, and now she was just about to get fired from this one.

"Hello?" came a friendly voice.

Good. It was Mr. Throgmorton. "Hello, sir. This is Courtney from the Curly Bay Pet Hotel and Rescue. I'm afraid Sir Glitter has gone missing."

There was a long pause on the other end of the line, right before it exploded. "Missing? You've got to be kidding me? A dog doesn't just go missing!"

"I know, and we're still trying to figure out how it happened." Courtney knew it didn't really matter how it happened. She'd be blamed simply because she was new. That was how the world worked.

"We're talking about a very expensive dog, young lady. And not just expensive to buy. No, no. There's all his training to consider, as well as all his blue ribbons! He's a pedigreed champion!"

"I understand that but—"

"There is no but!" Mr. Throgmorton yelled back. "You must find him, and find him now!"

Courtney was just about to assure him they were doing everything in their power when she heard a screeching sound in the background. It was Mrs. Throgmorton. If the kind gentleman, could react this badly, Courtney could only imagine what it would be like to see what his wife was doing.

Courtney didn't have to wait long to find out, considering the screeching over the phone was matched by the screeching of Mrs. Throgmorton's tires as she came careering into the parking lot half an hour later. She slammed the door and marched in, her fists curled at her sides and her puffy hair slightly off-kilter from the fast drive.

Ms. O'Donnell pulled up right behind her. She got out calmly and walked inside as though this were a regular day on the job.

Courtney wished she could shrink herself down to the size of a flea and hop away instead of dealing with this, but there was no choice but to bear down and get it over with. "Hi, Mrs. Throgmorton. I'm glad you're here. I want you to know we're doing everything—"

"You!" the older woman hissed, pointing a bejeweled finger at Courtney as she advanced on her. "You lost my baby! You are responsible for losing the most important thing in my entire life!"

Courtney gaped at her. She'd expected to be blamed, but not to this degree. "You must understand that this was simply an accident. The last I knew the back door was locked. The bolt was done, but—"

"No! I don't want to hear another single word from you unless it's that you've found Sir Glitter! You're going to pay for this, girl!"

Girl? She was thirty-two years old! Courtney glanced at Ms. O'Donnell.

The owner seemed to suddenly realize she should be involved in some capacity. "Courtney and Jessi have looked all over the property, and we've notified Animal Control."

"Animal Control?" Mrs. Throgmorton finally stopped pointing so that she could put the back of her hand to her forehead in a dramatic style. "You're suggesting my poor little baby might get picked up by *them*? He can't be snatched up with one of those catch poles and shoved into a crate! He's far too sensitive for that!"

"They only use those in certain situations, and I'm sure Sir Glitter wouldn't be one of them," Courtney corrected, trying desperately to get some sort of hold on the situation. "And it might not even be Animal Control who finds him. We'll continue to look constantly until he turns up, and maybe he's just wandered into someone's yard."

"Yes, someone who'll see an expensive dog and keep it as their own! I know how it works! But that's saying he's actually wandered off. I don't trust you, Miss…Miss…"

Courtney tried hard not to roll her eyes. "Cain. Courtney Cain." There. Now the woman had her name, and she could do with it what she wanted.

"Sounds about right, like someone you can't trust," Mrs. Throgmorton snapped. "I know you're responsible, Miss Cain, and I'll use every resource I have to find my dog and prove that you stole him!"

"Wait. What?" Courtney glanced at the other women, wondering if she'd heard this correctly. She'd expected to be blamed, but not to be accused of stealing. "I did nothing of the sort."

"We'll just see about that, won't we?" Mrs. Throgmorton threw her chin in the air and spread her shoulders as she turned to strut out the door.

The silence in the room felt like the aftermath of a hurricane. "This is insane," Courtney whispered.

"I'm sure it'll all come out in the wash," Ms. O'Donnell said flippantly.

"Have you had something like this happen before? With a missing animal?" Courtney knew cats and dogs wandered off all the time, but not usually ones who were supposed to be in cages. Still, someone must've slipped off the leash at some point.

Ms. O'Donnell slowly shook her head. "No, I can't say that it has."

"Wonderful." Courtney turned on her heel and went to her desk. This was officially the longest workday in all of history.

CHAPTER FIVE

When she got back to her apartment that evening, Courtney collapsed onto her couch and looked around. The flat was a nice enough one, with a picture window in the front living room, an open floor plan that led to the dining room and kitchen toward the back, and a wide patio door that looked out over a little rectangle of concrete and a patch of grass she could call her own. The short hallway led to the bathroom, the laundry closet, and her bedroom.

Everything, from the walls to the curtains to the carpet, was beige. It should've been relaxing to look at after such a busy and stressful day, but it only made her more anxious. She'd moved in a hurry, and she hadn't yet had time to turn this place into her home. There were stacks of boxes in the corners, reminding her of all that hadn't yet been unpacked. Dishes, knickknacks, and even clothes awaited her attention.

She frowned down at the dark blue polo she'd put on that morning. It certainly wasn't dark blue anymore. It was covered in every color and length of cat and dog hair imaginable, from creamy white fluffy bits that could very well belong to Sir Glitter to dark orange lines from one of the rescue cats. With a sigh, she got up to change her shirt, vowing never to wear dark colors to work again.

The doorbell rang just as she was about to find something for dinner. Courtney thought she might find a neighbor or the landlady, but instead it was a large man with slumping shoulders. His posture matched the lugubrious look on his long face, and he blinked sleepily at Courtney as she answered the door. "Detective Fletcher, Curly Bay P.D.," he said slowly. Television cops always flashed their badges quickly, but this guy acted as though it was too heavy to hold up. "I'd like to ask you a few questions about the missing Pomeranian from your place of employment."

Courtney held the door open wider to let him in. This was ridiculous, but there wasn't any getting around it. "Please, come in and have a seat."

Detective Fletcher slowly rolled in, looking around the room. "Nice place you got here. Just moved in?" He slowly lowered himself to the couch.

"Just a couple of days ago, yes. I moved here from the city to take the job at the pet hotel." Which she might be on the verge of losing. Ms. O'Donnell hadn't said that yet, but Courtney wouldn't be surprised to find a pink slip waiting on her sometime soon.

"I see. Curly Bay is a nice quiet town, nothing like the city." He swiped a hand over his face, looking like he might fall asleep if he let himself relax just a little too far back into the cushions.

"Am I being charged? Should I have a lawyer present?" Courtney perched herself on a nearby chair, not feeling nearly as easy as Detective Fletcher looked.

He gave her half a shrug. "You're always welcome to get a lawyer if you want, but there aren't any charges. Yet."

"Yet?"

Fletcher let out a long sigh. "We're talking about Mrs. Throgmorton. If you just moved to town, then you don't really know her well, but she's the sort who likes to throw her weight around."

"Yes, I gathered that."

"She's the only reason I'm even here. We don't currently have any evidence to suggest the dog was stolen, but Mrs. Throgmorton won't stop calling the station until she believes we're doing something proactive about this missing dog. As I'm sure she told you, she thinks you stole it."

Now it was Courtney's turn to sigh, something she'd done a lot of in the past few hours. "I gathered that, as well."

"I don't hear a little dog yapping in the bedroom somewhere, so that's a good sign," the detective chuckled with a dry wheeze. "Now, then. You just tell me what happened."

"Okay." She'd been going over and over it in her head, anyway, so maybe it'd be good to get it all off her chest. "I was at work. It was my first day, and Ms. O'Donnell—"

"That the owner?"

"Yes. Ms. O'Donnell had shown me around—"

"The blonde, right?"

"Yes. She—"

"I talked to her down at the pet hotel. She's really pretty. Do you know if she's married?"

Courtney had very little patience left to lose. "Detective Fletcher, I believe you said you wanted to hear my side of the story. If you'd prefer I play matchmaker for you, we'll have to do that some other time."

"Right, right. Sorry. Go on." He rolled his hand through the air to encourage her.

"Anyway. Ms. O'Donnell had shown me around and given me a little bit of information about how the place is run, and she told me to make sure the back door was locked. I know it was when we talked about it, and—are you going to write any of this down?" Courtney had never had to deal with the police directly, but the ones on TV always took out a little notebook to scribble in while they were interviewing suspects or witnesses.

Fletcher jabbed his finger at his temple. "I've got a mind like a steel trap, Miss Cain. Don't worry."

She was worried, but she did her best to recount the day. There wasn't much to tell, save that the dog had been there and then he was gone. "Mrs. Throgmorton was very upset when she arrived, which I completely understand, but I think this whole idea of blaming me is a bit over the top."

He didn't tell her to stick to the facts, so maybe Detective Fletcher wasn't like the screen cops at all. "We need some real evidence to get much further. I talked with Ms. O'Donnell about the security system at the hotel and the broken camera, so of course that's not going to get us anywhere."

"Are you saying I don't need to worry?" Courtney very much wanted to put all this behind her.

Fletcher scratched his jaw. "I can't tell you that. It could all just blow over, or maybe not. Since we're dealing with a very influential couple, I think you'd be smart to get an attorney.

"Okay. Thanks." Disappointed, she saw Detective Fletcher out with a promise to call him if she thought of anything else pertinent.

After heating up a can of soup for dinner, Courtney decided to distract herself by unpacking her things. These boxes were going to turn into permanent fixtures if she didn't attack them right away. They'd been stacked randomly, and most of them weren't even in the right room. After going through a box of bath towels and another of coffee mugs, she found a random carton of paperwork, magazines, and books.

She recognized the contents as what had been scattered across the top of her coffee table when she'd scraped them all together, in a hurry to get everything loaded onto the moving van.

An issue of *For the Love of Dogs* sat on top. Courtney had picked it up at the grocery checkout to help her study up on everything currently happening in the dog world. Ms. O'Donnell had been so quick to call her back and offer her the job that Courtney hadn't even had a chance to read it before she moved. She tossed it onto the coffee table, knowing it would still be a good source of information.

The magazine slid across the glass surface and hung on for just a moment as it teetered on the edge before tumbling to the floor. Sighing in frustration, Courtney moved to pick it up. It'd fallen open to a picture of someone familiar.

"Sir Glitter presides from his first-place podium at the Happy Pet Purebred Show last month," Courtney read out loud from the photo's caption. She skimmed over the rest of the article, which was mostly about the show itself instead of the winning canine. "Huh. So he's a show dog. No real surprise." Courtney had no doubt Mrs. Throgmorton tried to show off Sir Glitter as much as possible.

She was just about to put the magazine down when she noticed the other competitors in the photo. Just behind Sir Glitter sat a rather large and curly dog, a Labradoodle. Courtney gasped as she noticed the dog's handler, who was just getting him settled on his second-place podium. Pulling the magazine closer to be doubly sure, Courtney saw the bald man with the ridiculously curly mustache who'd been at the kennel asking about Sir Glitter.

"Odd," she muttered as she tapped the magazine on the edge of the coffee table. It was strange that the man had come to the Curly Bay Pet Hotel and Rescue to ask for a Pomeranian specifically? Perhaps he'd seen Sir Glitter best his own beast in the show and wanted to change breeds, or maybe he knew that particular Pom was currently in residence.

"If they know each other through the show circuit, which would make sense, it wouldn't be too far-fetched an idea that Mr. Labradoodle had been following the Throgmortons and knew exactly where they kept their boy during the day. He could've stolen Sir Glitter as revenge, helping ensure his own blue ribbon at the next show." Excited, Courtney scraped through the rest of the box, quickly finding a notepad. She dug a pen out of her purse and began making a list. Just to be sure she didn't miss anything, Courtney flipped to the next page. Sir Glitter was on it, but as a spokesdog for some sort of pet insurance policy.

She didn't know the man's real name, so she simply wrote 'Mr. Labradoodle' at the top of a clean sheet, listing her theories that pointed toward him underneath. Courtney tapped her pen on her chin, wondering if there was anyone else who might have a reason to take Sir Glitter.

It was made that much harder by the fact that she didn't really know anybody in Curly Bay. She'd just moved there, and the only people she'd really met besides her landlady were from work, and Courtney highly doubted she'd have any interest in the fluffy little dog.

Biting her lip, Courtney added Ms. O'Donnell's name to the list. She seemed like a nice enough woman, but it was odd that she'd made specific reference to the back door. It was even odder that she'd also decided to leave as soon as she'd finished giving Courtney a tour of the place. As Courtney wrote, she also remembered that the pet hotel owner hadn't bothered defending her in front of Mrs. Throgmorton.

Her head was starting to throb as she tried to figure this all out. She was always praised for her problem-solving skills when she worked for Miller and Martinez, but those problems were different. When she'd been faced with issues like coming up with a new mascot for an insurance company or which jingle they should use for a fast food restaurant, she knew instinctively what the right answer was. Transforming herself from a marketing consultant to a detective wasn't going to be easy.

CHAPTER SIX

Although she wouldn't have thought it possible, Courtney was even more nervous when she showed up at the Curly Bay Pet Hotel and Rescue for her second day of work than she'd been for the first. She had no idea what was waiting for her on the other side of those glass front doors. Ms. O'Donnell might let her go, leaving her to either break her lease on the new flat or to find a new job in Curly Bay. Worse, everything might continue as usual until Detective Fletcher showed up to arrest her. She wondered what jail was like in a small coastal town like this. She'd never needed to know much about legal matters before.

There was no telling until she got up her gumption and went inside, though, and so she did. Nobody jumped out from behind a chair to arrest her, and Ms. O'Donnell wasn't waiting around to give her a pink slip. In fact, the first thing Courtney noticed was that she didn't see the owner around at all.

"Hey, Jessi." Courtney tried to sound as casual as possible, despite the events of the previous day. "Have you seen Ms. O'Donnell this morning? I wanted to ask her about a few things."

Jessi brushed her short dark hair out of her eyes as she got the main computer booted up for the day. "No, not yet. But she doesn't usually come in until later anyway. If she even comes in at all."

"Is there a reason she doesn't spend much time here? I mean, if she's the owner, I'd think she'd want to be pretty involved." Especially with a brand-new manager who'd lost an expensive dog and been accused of stealing it on the very first day. Courtney had no idea what kind of relationship Ms. O'Donnell had with the rest of the staff, so this question could be out of line. She was starting not to care.

The rescue worker shrugged as she straightened a stack of paperwork and turned on the printer. "I don't know. That's just how it's always been, at least since I've worked here."

"Gotcha." Courtney felt awkward, not yet into that comfortable swing of working a job she knew like the back of her hand. She wondered if it would ever change for her. "I know I didn't get much of a chance to help you yesterday. Is there anything you need from me?"

"Nah, at least not right now. I might need some help with walking later in the afternoon, though."

"Can do." Courtney threaded her way through the reception area and into her office, sitting down at her desk. She'd hardly had her backside in the chair at all the previous day, and she figured she ought to take the opportunity while she could. The top drawer held a typical array of pens, pencils, and little notepads with the shelter's logo emblazoned across the top. The next drawer was full of file folders. Rifling through them, Courtney realized they were employee records.

This was perfect! If anyone here had a criminal record that might point to a motive for stealing Sir Glitter, she could give Detective Fletcher some information that would point him in a different direction. In a way, it felt like she was betraying her own employees. She didn't want to accuse anyone falsely, because she certainly hadn't enjoyed being accused herself. However, desperate times called for desperate measures. Besides, she was the manager. She had every right to look though these files.

The influx of doggie daycare folks hadn't started yet, so Courtney flipped open the first file she came across. Dora Grant's name was written along the tab in an unfamiliar handwriting, possibly Ms. O'Donnell's, but more likely the previous manager, considering how little the owner had to do with her own business. Inside, however, Courtney realized this file had probably been created even before the previous manager. Dora had been with the Curly Bay Pet Hotel and Rescue back when it was simply a rescue. Courtney would need to look up some dates, but she wouldn't be surprised if Dora's hire date coincided with the day the doors first opened. Her resume, which included some good references from local veterinarians and a pet grooming school, was clipped inside. Courtney looked through everything, finding all the typical information she expected. There was no reference to any record, and whoever had hired Dora had done a criminal background check. The woman had been clean as of the day she'd been hired, but something might've happened after that.

"Hey!"

Courtney reeled back in her chair in surprise. The seat tipped further back than seemed safe, causing her to fling out her arms for balance. The file folder and all its contents went scattering to the floor underneath her desk. She dove to her knees to scoop them all back up again.

"I didn't mean to scare you, but I called your name several times." It was Dora, and she advanced across the room. "I'll help you get those."

"No! I mean, it's fine. I've got it. I was just in my own little world. I guess I need to get some coffee going." With shaking hands, Courtney stuffed the papers back into the file, not even paying attention to the order or if they were facing the right direction, and crammed the folder back into the desk. "What did you need me for?"

"I was going to tell you we need to put in a supply order. I'm getting low on several types of shampoo, and I need a new set of nail trimmers for large dogs." Dora crossed to the coffee pot and poured a cup for herself, but she didn't offer one to her manager.

Courtney tried not to take offense, but that was difficult. She'd get her own coffee later when she'd calmed down. Right now, it was better to sit at her desk with her hands folded on the wooden surface so Dora wouldn't know how shaken she was. "Sure. Is there a specific company we order from?"

Dora stirred a heaping spoon of sugar into her coffee and rolled her eyes. "It's all right there in that binder."

"Oh. Right." Courtney was fairly sure Ms. O'Donnell hadn't said anything about that particular binder. She flipped it open. The phone number and website were written on the inside of the cover, and a catalog had been fitted into the metal rings. Behind that were numerous invoices from previous orders. "What kind of shampoo did you need?"

The sigh that Dora let out was long and irritable. "Never mind. I'll just take care of it myself."

Courtney frowned. She hadn't exactly been high on the food chain at her marketing firm, but she was certain nobody had been that disrespectful toward each other. Other than, of course, Sam firing her, but that was a different matter. "Dora, I know it's difficult to get used to a new manager. I'm doing my best. But I won't ever know what you need from me if you don't give me a chance."

The woman's face pinched together. She wasn't convinced. "Maybe we wouldn't have to deal with any of this if Ms. O'Donnell had just hired from within." Dora turned and stomped out of the room, sloshing some of the coffee over the side of her cup and not even bothering to clean it up.

Ah! So that was Dora's problem! She was angry because she hadn't been promoted to manager when the position came open. Although Courtney hadn't brought her list of suspects to work with her, she made a mental note to add Dora to it.

Now that she was alone again, she quickly flipped through the employee file on Jessi. It wasn't nearly as old, but it didn't have anything incriminating. There was another folder for Ms. O'Donnell, but it only listed emergency contact information.

While she still had a little time on her hands, Courtney quickly looked through the computer system, hoping to cross-reference something about Pomeranians, Labradoodles, or show dogs. She studied the Throgmortons' information, listing them as living on Hummingbird Lane. There were tons of large invoices, all promptly paid, for the numerous services Sir Glitter required. Courtney stifled a giggle as she saw that the spoiled dog even got mud baths and foot massages. "They treat him better than I've ever treated myself," she muttered. There was no record of any previous trouble with either the dog or the owners, and she didn't find any Labradoodles in the system.

Her search hadn't given her much to go on. There was nothing left but to continue on with her day, hoping she could manage to at least do most of her job right.

CHAPTER SEVEN

Courtney stepped into the attached garage and pushed the button, watching the door rise and let the morning sunshine in. It'd been a relatively uneventful last couple of days at the shelter, with no break in the case or even word from Detective Fletcher. Courtney now had the day off, and she was going to take advantage of it.

The air was thick with humidity as she pulled out of the garage, but the sunshine and a gentle breeze made the late spring day absolutely beautiful. With no appointments or real agenda, Courtney toured her neighborhood. The few blocks surrounding her place were all full of more apartments, some of them small duplexes and quadplexes and a few others larger brick edifices. These gave way to little bungalows and ranches with nice yards, perfect for small families. The streets were all perfect grids and named after trees and historical figures. Children played on the sidewalks or even right out in the streets, skittering out of the way of oncoming traffic and running right back out onto the pavement once the car had passed. Dogs barked behind fences, and people lifted a hand in a friendly wave as they watered their lawns or picked up the paper.

On the outskirts of town, Courtney found a neighborhood completely unlike what she'd already seen. The streets wound around in confusing curlicues and cul-de-sacs, all named after birds. Large homes sat proudly on massive lots of green grass, proudly sporting far too many gables or ridiculous columns. A golf course with a country club was yet another stretch of greenery, the flags fluttering in the breeze. It was all nice, but Courtney couldn't help noticing that there was nobody in sight. Wherever the kids were, they'd been kept indoors. The only people she saw outside were from lawn service companies, hired to mow the grass. All the cars were parked in garages, without any left out on the street. It was an entirely different world here where the wealthy folks lived.

As she headed downtown, Courtney realized that the two sides of the Curly Bay Pet Hotel and Rescue were basically the same way. On one end were those who could afford all the luxuries in life. Their owners were never faced with bathing, grooming, and nail clipping, because they could pay someone else to do it for them. The dogs and cats had fancy collars and microchips, although they were never let outside without being directly supervised. Courtney wouldn't doubt if some of them had never gotten to go outside at all.

For the rescues, they were just getting by doing the best they could. Jessi had told her the story of Gus, a pit bull who'd been found digging through a dumpster in desperate hope of a meal. Someone had brought him to the shelter instead, where he got a bowl full of kibble that he was always exceptionally grateful for. Gus always gave a little lick on the back of the hand to whomever happened to fill his bowl. There were plenty of others like him, too, dogs and cats who didn't have to have anything fancy as long as they just had a roof over their heads.

"Don't start thinking about that," she said to herself as she found one of the downtown parking lots that served most of the buildings along Main Street.

"Then you'll start bringing them all home, and the landlady won't like that at all." Mrs. Peabody had been very straightforward about her pet policy.

A charcoal gray sedan pulled into the parking lot as she was getting out of her car. Courtney could swear she'd seen it several times already that morning, but there was no telling how many people drove something similar. She walked on.

She'd noted when she'd first come to Curly Bay that the main downtown area was full of old shops. These were built up close to the road, huddling against each other as they overlooked the street. Many of the buildings looked to be over a century old, some of them with fancy brickwork that modern contractors simply didn't do. Here and there, an old sign that had been painted directly on the building decades before was left to fade out on its own, even though it had nothing to do with the business that currently resided there. Courtney wanted to get to know this town as much as possible if she was going to live here, and this seemed like the perfect start.

Her first stop was a little bakery. After purchasing a blueberry cheesecake muffin and a cup of coffee, she sat at a table to enjoy her snack. Courtney had spent plenty of time in the city, so she was used to people coming and going without paying attention to her. It was clear that wasn't the case in Curly Bay. A man at the corner table kept lowering his newspaper to look at her with his steely gray eyes.

Polishing off her muffin, she moved next door to an antique shop. The owner practically bounced out from behind the counter, even though the store was crowded enough that bouncing would be a terrible idea. "Hi, there! Can I help you? Are you looking for anything in particular? I've got a great selection of vintage coffee mugs."

"No, thanks. I'm just here to look around. I'm new in town." Courtney skirted around an antique dining table that'd been set up in the middle of the room with a very fancy tea set.

"Oh, really? That's exciting! Where are you from?" The clerk followed her as they moved among various china cabinets and rolltop desks.

"I just moved here from the city."

"Now, *that's* interesting. Don't get me wrong." He held up his hands to keep her from making any hasty judgements. "I love Curly Bay. I've lived here almost my entire life. I just can't figure out why anybody would want to move here from somewhere else, especially someplace exciting like the city. So many things to see and do!"

Courtney didn't respond, not wanting to get into the whole story about getting fired. She kept her focus on a lamp with a tasseled shade that she had no intention of buying.

"So, where in these parts did you settle down?"

"Oh, just a little apartment for now." The guy seemed nice enough, but she wasn't going to give him every detail of her life.

"I see. Are you needing any furniture? Do have a particular style? I've got some great mid-century modern pieces in the back."

Courtney secretly hoped that not everyone in Curly Bay was as friendly and helpful as this man. "I'm good for now. Just looking around and getting to know the area."

"Well, I—" The clerk seemed as though he was going to make another suggestion about his inventory when the bell over the door rang. "I'm going to go see who that is. You feel free to browse around, and holler if there's anything you need!" He disappeared through the congested aisles. A moment later, Courtney could hear him greeting the next customer. "Hi, there! Can I help you? Are you looking for anything in particular?"

She stifled a laugh.

When she managed to sneak back by the counter without the clerk noticing her, Courtney spotted the other customer. He was a short gentleman with narrow shoulders and dark hair. Though she couldn't quite see his face, she was certain it was the same man who'd been staring at her back in the bakery. Courtney left, figuring that was just the way things worked in small towns.

But then she saw the same man sitting in the lobby at the bank as she finished up opening a new checking account. He'd positioned himself behind a potted ficus, but there'd been no mistaking those cold eyes that stared at her between the leaves.

"You're just seeing things," she whispered to herself as she walked across the street to a video rental store. "You've had a rough week here, and it's getting to you. Everything is fine. As long as he doesn't follow you back to your apartment, everything is fine."

She truly wanted to convince herself, but it was easier said than done as he lurked through the aisles of the video store, always one genre behind her. At one point, she thought she saw him take a little notepad out of his jacket pocket and scribble something down. It appeared that he is keeping track of the movies titles she picked up.

When she'd checked out, Courtney stood at the corner of the building and took out her phone. She was in full view of anyone who drove by on the busy street, and even the video clerk would be able to see her through the wide window on the front of the building.

"Detective Fletcher," answered a sleepy voice.

"Hi, this is Courtney Cain."

Silence greeted her on the other end of the phone.

"The one Mrs. Throgmorton accused of stealing her dog?" she reminded him.

"Oh. Oh, yeah. Right. What can I do for you?"

"You can tell me why you're having me tailed," she asserted.

"Excuse me?"

Courtney kept an eye on the door to the video rental store. The man who'd been following her hadn't come out yet because she hadn't moved away. She had no doubt he'd come out those doors as soon as she stepped off the sidewalk. "You're having me followed, aren't you?"

"No. Why would I do that?"

Did she really have to tell him how his job worked? "To find evidence. To arrest me. I don't know. You tell me."

"Miss Cain, I'm not having anyone follow you. The Curly Bay Police Department is pretty severely understaffed, and I can't say that we have the resources for that sort of thing."

She frowned. As aggravated as the idea of being followed made her, she didn't really like Detective Fletcher's answer any better. "Then how do you explain the same man following me into four different businesses?"

His sigh came through the phone as a long breath of static. "Miss Cain, you said you moved here from the city, right?"

"Right."

"So, you're not used to small town life. You're going to run into the same people at the hardware store and at the ice cream shop. Plus, you're probably feeling a little paranoid—"

"I'm *not* paranoid!" In fact, she thought she was holding up rather well, considering the circumstances. "I know what I saw."

"The brain can play some nasty little tricks," Fletcher countered. "Why, I've seen people turn themselves in simply because they were tired of wondering when they'd be arrested for whatever crime they committed. Waiting is a terrible thing, whether you're innocent or guilty."

She rolled her eyes. The only waiting that was truly terrible right now was waiting to see if Detective Fletcher would shut up anytime soon. "Okay. Fine. Thanks, then." She hung up, hoping that she never needed the Curly Bay Police Department for anything.

The idea of being followed, whether it was someone from the police department or otherwise, made Courtney a bit sick to her stomach. She charged down the sidewalk, no longer appreciating the sun on her shoulders or the breeze in her dark hair. Instead, she dove into a burger joint at the end of the block and ordered a soda.

When she sat down in a booth near the back, she noticed that the man had followed her yet again. At some point, he'd seen her step away from the video rental store and shadowed her through town, apparently sticking on a horrible fake mustache along the way. It stuck out too far from his upper lip as he tried to sip his own soda and look casually out the window.

Courtney stewed, wondering how she was going to address this. She didn't know anybody here. Detective Fletcher wasn't going to help her. Her friends and family were too far away to call. She was on her own in this little diner.

She took a few more pulls on her soda, watching the mysterious man in her peripheral vision while thinking about her life. When she was only seventeen, she'd moved out of her parents' home and off to college. It was a scary thing, but she'd gotten through it. As soon as she had her degree in her hand, she'd landed the job with Miller and Martinez. Courtney had been incredibly intimidated by the big corporate office, the executives in their expensive suits, and the pressure to perform, but she'd done well. She'd been let go, but the reason on her pink slip was that they were downsizing. Nobody had ever come out and said she hadn't done her job well. Even losing that job was an obstacle on its own. She'd found a new one, and even though it was a rough start, she was on her way to the next chapter in her life.

"Well, then. No reason to sit around and be a victim." Courtney stood up from her booth. She crushed the paper soda cup in her hand and shoved it into the trash can. Her steps were firm and even as she walked over to the man's table and slammed her hands down. "Why are you following me?" she demanded.

"Excuse me?" The man fanned his fingers out on his chest as though offended. "I'm not following anyone." The corner of his mustache began to peel up.

"You're seriously going to sit there and lie to my face? You parked your car in the same lot as mine. That's fine. I can understand that. But you were at the bakery, the bank, the video store, and now here. Something is up."

"Listen, lady. I have rights. You can't just charge up to me and start yelling at me." The end of his mustache had come completely off now, and it dangled in front of his lips as he spoke.

"Would you care to explain the fake fur on your face, then?" She was tempted to reach out and yank it right off his lip, but she drew the line at touching a stranger's face.

"Martin, are you harassing my customers again?" Courtney hadn't even seen the woman appear at her side. She was an older woman, and she'd squeezed her ample curves into the red and white uniform of the restaurant. Her nametag indicated her as Sherry, and she jammed her fist onto her hip like she meant business.

The man shrunk down into his seat. "I'm not harassing anyone. I was just sitting here minding my own business."

"And I'd venture to guess you've been 'minding your business' all over town. You know how I feel about you doing your private investigating in here." Sherry raised her eyebrows and frowned, daring the man to challenge her.

"Wait, you're a private investigator?" Courtney had made all sorts of guesses about the man, most recently that he was stalking her or waiting to rob her.

"Martin Duffy, P.I.," the man responded as he straightened in his seat. He shrunk back a little and glanced from Courtney to Sherry and back again. "Why are you laughing?"

"Because..." She was giggling too hard to give him a full answer, and she smacked her own thigh at the humor of it all. "Because you're terrible!"

Sherry started to giggle as well, and then they were both laughing fully, tears running down their faces.

Martin cleared his throat. "For someone who gets offended at being followed, perhaps you should try having someone laugh at you. It's very rude." The fake mustache jiggled across his lips once again, making the women laugh harder. He ripped it off, leaving a large red rectangle under his nose.

"I'm sorry," Courtney gasped. "I'm so sorry. You're right. I am being rude. But it's been a horrible week, and then you were following me. And the ficus at the bank, and that mustache, and oh!" She collapsed in a fit of laughter once again.

"And now you outright insult me to my face!" Martin stood up, lifting his chin in the air and squaring his shoulders. His efforts were countered by his diminutive size, and Courtney just wanted to laugh all over again.

Fortunately, Sherry had mostly regained her composure. "Martin here is the only private investigator in town," she explained. "He makes a living off of spying on people, or at least he tries to."

"I'm very gainfully employed at the moment," Martin argued.

Sherry didn't seem to care. "You can always call the police on him if he's harassing you. They can't do a whole lot as long as he's on public property, but they can at least shoo him off for the time being."

"I wasn't harassing anybody!" Martin repeated.

While the incompetent investigator had been hilarious, the truth of the situation hit Courtney like a ton of bricks. "The Throgmortons hired you, didn't they?"

Martin studied his fingernails. "I don't have to answer that."

"That's a yes," Sherry supplied.

"Hey!"

But as far as Courtney was concerned, Sherry was right. She pointed a finger at the little man's chest. "Good. Then you just go right ahead and follow me. You can waste all your time and their money while you traipse along behind me on my errands, and then you can trot right back over to them and tell them that I don't have their dog!"

She started to leave, but then she turned back around. "Sherry? Thank you. I'll be sure to come back." Courtney left the two of them to deal with each other while she made her way back to her car and then home. She had no interest in visiting any other local establishments at the moment.

CHAPTER EIGHT

"Good evening, Mr. and Mrs. Throgmorton. I just wanted to stop by and ask if we could work this all out." Courtney studied her smile in the mirror. It was too fake, and she couldn't blame herself. She didn't feel like smiling at all.

Stepping out of the bathroom and grabbing her purse, she once again opened the garage door. She watched carefully for any sign of Martin Duffy's car, but everything in the neighborhood seemed normal as far as she could tell. Maybe she'd scared him off for a little while. Inept as the man was, she still wasn't crazy about the idea of anyone lurking in the shadows while she went about her daily business. She checked her mirrors several times as she wound her way through town, noting any vehicle that happened to be behind her, but nobody followed her to her destination.

Courtney double-checked the address she'd written down before pulling into the driveway. The house was one of the largest in the upper-class development. It borrowed architectural features from several eras, sporting gables, dormers, and covered porches. The mix of deep gray vinyl siding and stone brought it into the modern age, paired with crisp white trim and a circle driveway. There was no sign of a single weed in the yard, and the hedges had been trimmed until each leaf was tamed. As she walked up to the double doors, Courtney wasn't sure if she should expect the owner of the home or a butler.

The bell rang long and deep from within the home. Once again, Courtney tried to go over what she was going to say. She knew from having to prepare for meetings with big executives that having certain phrasing ready to go always helped. The conversation never went exactly as planned, but it still left her feeling prepared. She hoped she could tap into that old talent as Mr. Throgmorton answered the door. "Good evening, Mr. Throgmorton. I just wanted to stop by and ask if we could work this out like adults. I've brought the two of you some flowers." Courtney thrust out the bouquet of dahlias, daisies, and tiny little roses that she'd picked up at the small grocery store at the end of her street.

Instead of his suit and cowboy hat, Mr. Throgmorton wore a short-sleeved button-down and khakis. He frowned past the flowers at her. "We're not interested in talking to you."

This was one of the responses she'd prepared for. "I recognize that, but I think if you just give me a chance, you'll see that this was just a big misunderstanding." She smiled and pressed the flowers at him once again, taking a step toward the door as though she might come in. She would never dare step foot over his threshold without an invitation, but she could be a little pushy if she needed to be.

"No. I'm asking you to leave, and if you don't, I'll call the police." He pointed back the way she'd come, as though she were just a bad stray dog.

"Who is it, Ken?" called a voice from another room.

"Nobody, dear." Mr. Throgmorton began closing the door.

"At least call off your private investigator," Courtney insisted, not willing to just give this all up. She'd taken a lot of time out of her day to make this happen. While she'd already seen the Throgmortons' address in the records at the shelter, she made sure she could find them easily enough online so that nobody could accuse her of abusing her managerial power. She'd planned out every situation that could arise, and she'd even intended to ask them about Mr. Labradoodle. Maybe if they knew their rival had been inquiring about Sir Glitter, it would take some of the pressure off her. She couldn't just let this go because they refused to speak to her!

"It can't be nobody," Mrs. Throgmorton responded to her husband from within the house, her high heels clacking closer. "If it's those girls selling cookies, I want to get some of the peanut butter ones."

"No, Janice. Nothing like that." Mr. Throgmorton shut the door.

Mrs. Throgmorton pulled it open again. Her face instantly transformed from one of pleasant expectation to one of pure hatred. "You," she snarled. "Unless you're here to return my baby, then I suggest you leave right now."

She'd already pretty much heard that part. Courtney held out the flowers once again. "I brought these for you, hoping we could sit down and talk."

"What is this, a hostage negotiation?" Mrs. Throgmorton snatched the bouquet out of Courtney's hand. "And I'm allergic to dahlias. Ah-choo!" She let out a very fake sneeze.

"I'm sorry. I didn't know, I just—" Her words were cut off as the soft, cold plop of a dahlia hit her face.

Mrs. Throgmorton snatched another flower out of the bouquet and sent it flying. "Don't tell me how sorry you are until you come back here with my little dog!" A rose shot out of her hands. "You're the most irresponsible, horrible person I've ever met!"

Mr. Throgmorton pressed himself against the doorway to avoid getting caught up in his wife's wrath.

Courtney put up a hand to deflect a daisy as she realized nobody ever did anything to stop Mrs. Throgmorton. They simply let her do her thing because she was so wealthy. It irritated her that someone should be able to get away with almost anything just because she had a few extra dollars in her pocket. "One of these days—ow! One of these days, someone is going to stand up and stop you from being so rotten to everyone."

"Are you threatening me?" the woman shrieked. "Ken, call the police! Tell them to get this crazy woman off my steps!"

Considering the speed with which Courtney was backing away to avoid the barraging bouquet, she highly doubted the police would be on Mrs. Throgmorton's side. Then again, Detective Fletcher had bothered to interview both herself and Ms. O'Donnell just so Mrs. Throgmorton would leave him alone. It was clear Fletcher didn't do anything unless he absolutely had to, which said a lot.

Giving up, Courtney retreated to her car and got in, making sure the windows were rolled up before she headed out of the driveway. So much for working it out with the Throgmortons. He was like a little boy not wanting to let any girls into the fort, and she was like some high school mean girl who couldn't stand anybody that didn't bow to her decisions and opinions. That certainly didn't leave any room for asking about Mr. Labradoodle.

When she got home, she dialed up her Mom. "Hey, Mom."

"Hi, honey! How are things going down there in Curly Bay?" The sound of a barking dog came through the phone.

"Did you get a dog?"

"Oh, no. I'm just out for a walk. I brought my headset with me so I could listen to some music, though, so we're all set. Tell me how everything's going."

Courtney puffed up her cheeks and let out long breath as she turned on the kettle to make herself a cup of tea. "You know how when I got fired from the marketing firm you said something about it being a new opportunity or a new chance at life? Something like that?"

"Yes."

"Well, it was really just a new opportunity for me to mess up." Courtney took down her favorite mug and dug around in one of the moving boxes labeled 'kitchen' for some honey.

"It can't be that bad! Hi, Phyllis! Yes, it really is a beautiful day!"

Courtney gave a half smile as she envisioned her mother running into friendly neighbors while out walking. It was a sweet scene, one of suburban life and belonging. She didn't know how her mother had achieved that so easily, but she was from a different time. "My boss doesn't give me any direction on what I need to do, one of the staff members seems to hate my guts, a very expensive dog went missing, and the dog's owner is doing everything in her power to have me throw in jail."

Mrs. Cain gasped. "Honey, are you serious? Let me give you my cousin Arthur's number. He's a lawyer, and he might be able to help you out."

"No, Mom. I already thought about that, but he lives two hours away from me. If I need an attorney, I'll get one here." She poured the hot water over a chamomile tea bag, hoping it would be enough to settle her nerves. A spoonful of honey and a slice of lemon and she was on her way to sit on the back porch and try to enjoy the evening as much as possible.

"Okay, if you're sure. I don't remember what kind of law he deals with, but I'm sure he could at least point you in the right direction. Just keep it in mind." Birds chirped through the phone. "Now why would these people think you stole their dog?"

"Pure coincidence, really, plus the fact that it was my first day at the shelter and they knew everyone else already." Courtney had racked her brain to figure that out as well. She didn't know the Throgmortons prior to her job at the shelter, and she had no reason to want to steal Sir Glitter.

"You sound like it's getting you down, sugar, and I don't blame you. That's a tough position to be in, without a doubt. But I know you can get through it."

"I'm glad you think so, because I'm not so sure myself." She stared at the rows of privacy fencing that stretched away from the back of the property, sectioning off the grass like cubicle walls in an office building.

"Do you remember when you were a little girl and you'd missed a whole bunch of school while having your appendix out?"

"Unfortunately. That was awful." Courtney had missed a field trip because of that incident, which at the time had seemed like a very big deal.

"You thought so at first, and especially when Mrs. Gibson handed you a big envelope of homework that she expected you to make up. You were so upset, and you didn't think you could ever get through all that extra work."

"Yes, I remember." She could recall sitting at the foot of her bed, big tears plopping down onto the envelope as she contemplated having to spend the rest of her life making up for that hospital stay.

"But then you took everything out. You separated it all by subject until you had all these little stacks of paperwork on your floor. Then you decided you would go through and do a certain number of papers each day, starting with the one you wanted to do the least."

Courtney sipped her tea, enjoying the warmth of the liquid down her throat and the sweetness of the honey on her tongue. "I love you, Mom, but is there a point to this?"

"Of course! You weren't very old at the time—maybe ten or eleven—and you were faced with something that seemed absolutely impossible. Instead, you made a plan and worked through it. There were plenty of other times when you did something similar. I have no doubt you can use those skills of logic and order to make sense out of this mess, even if nobody else can."

"Well, I did start making a list of possible suspects," Courtney admitted. She took another sip of tea and noticed two figures bobbing up over a distance fence line. She realized after a minute that it was two kids jumping on a trampoline, their heads each popping into view for only a second or two before disappearing again.

"There you go," Mrs. Cain enthused. "You've already got a start. Just keep on going, and never take no for an answer. I know you can do it."

After a little more idle chitchat, the two of them got off the phone. Courtney's teacup was empty, and she thought a lot about what her mother had said. Logic and order could go a long way, but could they truly keep her out of hot water?

CHAPTER NINE

"Just tell them you'll handle it," she said to herself as she once again drove to the Curly Bay Pet Hotel and Rescue. "You're the one in charge, and you'll figure it out. And if there's anything you can't figure out, then you can call Ms. O'Donnell about it. She should've trained you. That's up to her, not the staff." She needed as much of a pep talk as she could get about the day, even if it was coming from herself.

She had no idea what the day would hold for her, but Courtney was determined to make it the best day yet at this job. The rest had been all pretty bad, although none of them had been worse than the day Sir Glitter had gone missing. At least, she knew, it couldn't get worse than that.

But when she pulled up in front of the building, she realized that it could. Alongside vehicles that belonged to Jessi and Dora, who always got there before everyone else, sat Ms. O'Donnell's vehicle. She was never in that early in the day, and that couldn't be a good sign, especially since a familiar gray sedan and a squad car were parked at the other end of the lot. Next to that was a very expensive car that could only belong to someone who was either here for hotel services or to see Courtney dragged off to jail.

"There she is! Finally!" exclaimed Martin Duffy as Courtney walked in the door. "We can get this show on the road. Detective?" He leaned over the counter to yell at Detective Fletcher.

The detective had a dreamy look on his face as he accepted a cup of coffee from Ms. O'Donnell. He smiled as he turned to the P.I. "Hmm? What's that? Oh, Miss Cain. How nice to see you this morning." He lifted his cup in greeting.

"Can we get on with this?" Mrs. Throgmorton demanded, folding her arms across her chest. She wore a cream pantsuit with a glittering diamond necklace, and her hair had been pulled back into a severe bun at the top of her head. Her husband put his arm protectively around her.

"What, exactly, is this?" Courtney hissed to Ms. O'Donnell. "A heads-up would've been nice, instead of just getting ambushed.

The owner gave a nonchalant shrug. "They've paid more bills here than anyone else in the place, and when they said they were bringing the police with them, I didn't really think I could say no."

That really wasn't her point, but Courtney was starting to learn that whatever point she was trying to make would always go straight over Ms. O'Donnell's head. She turned to the Throgmortons and Martin Duffy. "Let's get this over with, then."

The private investigator strode back and forth across the room, putting his hands behind his back and every now and then holding one finger up for emphasis. "I'm sure this will come as no surprise to any of you, but I've deduced that the person who stole Sir Glitter was none other than Courtney Cain!" He stopped and turned to point directly at her. "You have the dog. Admit it!"

She wanted to explode. She wanted to land a couple of punches to that sharp little chin of his and take him down, because she was sure she could take him. But Courtney knew that getting angry and losing her temper wasn't going to do her any good. She had something to prove here, but she didn't need to prove how much they'd all gotten under her skin in the meantime. "I don't, so I won't."

Detective Fletcher had returned to his normal gloomy state. "Do you have any evidence, Duffy?" He sipped his coffee, made a face, and then sipped it again.

"First, I have motive!" The investigator put his finger in the air once again. "Miss Cain was just fired from a job in the city at a marketing firm. According to the records I obtained, that job paid almost double what this one does, especially when including bonuses."

"I really don't see how my finances fit into this," Courtney remarked casually.

"Because you couldn't afford the lifestyle you were used to," Duffy replied. "You were miserable having to leave the city and come to this little one-horse town, but you saw a quick recovery in the form of a rather expensive show dog."

Courtney furrowed her brow at him. "Haven't you ever heard that phrase about how there's no such thing as a free puppy? Especially one like Sir Glitter. I could never afford the kind of upkeep he requires."

"But you were the one who put Sir Glitter in his kennel on the day in question. You were the one responsible for making sure the cage was latched. I understand that both his cage *and* the back door were open the day he went missing, and I understand that *you're* responsible for the security of the building. You were the one who put the dog away, and then he was gone!"

"I really don't think that can count as evidence," Courtney countered, looking to Detective Fletcher to see what he had to say about the matter.

The detective was too busy staring at Ms. O'Donnell to have paid any attention.

It was then that Courtney noticed the handcuffs dangling from the side of Fletcher's belt. Duffy and the Throgmortons might've called him here, but he was ready to make an arrest if necessary. Courtney didn't want to go to jail! Sure, she could get an attorney and get things straightened out. She probably wouldn't have to spend more than a single night. It wouldn't be the end of the world, but it certainly felt like it. The fact that she was now living in a small town that likely had a very busy rumor mill didn't help. As soon as those cuffs went on her wrists, everyone would know.

"Detective, you know as well as I do that she stole my dog. There's nobody else who would've done it!" Mrs. Throgmorton had a manicured finger pointed at Courtney.

"What about the guy with the Labradoodle?" Courtney blurted out. She flapped her hands in the air impatiently. "There's a man with a Labradoodle who came in the same day Sir Glitter went missing. He was asking about a Pomeranian, and he got really upset when I told him we didn't have any available for adoption. I noticed the same man's dog took second place behind Sir Glitter in a recent competition. Maybe he took the dog." She glanced from face to face, hoping for some spark of understanding.

Mr. Throgmorton shook his head emphatically. "That would be James Hathaway. He'd never do something like that!"

Courtney bit her lip. It was one thing to accuse a man who was a complete stranger and who wasn't there to witness it. The other suspects on her list worked here. If she brought up Dora or Ms. O'Donnell's name and they were innocent, her job could be very miserable in the future. If, that was, she even got to keep it.

"Okay," she said, remembering what her mother had told her about being logical and orderly. "Let's just slow down and think about the events of the day."

Mrs. Throgmorton rolled her eyes. "I don't have time for this!"

"Just give her a chance," Fletcher said. "It's not like we're making progress, anyway."

It wasn't exactly a vote of confidence, but she'd take what she could get. Courtney closed her eyes to help her remember. "It was my very first day of work. Ms. O'Donnell showed me around, and she specifically said the back door needed to be locked at all times because there's a problem with the security camera out back. She pointed to it, and I saw that the bolt had been slid shut."

"But then—" Duffy interrupted.

"Ssh! I'm thinking through this!" Courtney slowly unpacked the day in her mind, laying it all out and trying to see every angle. There had to be something she'd missed. "Mrs. Throgmorton came in to drop off Sir Glitter. I put him in his kennel, which I remember doing because she said it had to be a very specific kennel. I know I locked it, because the doors will come open a couple of inches if they aren't latched. Therefore, everything was latched when I was done putting Sir Glitter in his kennel."

"That only helps prove you weren't negligent," Mrs. Throgmorton asserted. "It doesn't clear you from stealing him."

"Then ask your little private investigator if he's seen me with a dog," Courtney challenged.

"You could've handed him off for someone else to hide until the coast was clear," came Mr. Throgmorton's reply.

Courtney's eyes widened as she studied the older man. "You came in that day! You said Sir Glitter didn't get his morning treat, and you wanted to make sure he got it."

"What?" Mrs. Throgmorton snapped. "How dare you! I always give him his treat! I would never forget!"

"Sorry, dear," he said humbly. "I just wanted to make sure he was taken care of."

"But you were the last one to see him!" Courtney concluded. "Only someone from the inside could open that back door. You lied about the treat and let him out!"

"That's absurd! Why would I steal my own dog?" Mr. Throgmorton flicked his fingers in the air to fling away the accusation.

"I don't know. Why would you bother coming all the way down here just to give him a treat? You could've waited until he got home, or just given us a call. There's nothing about any of this that makes sense!" Courtney's temper was starting to flare out, no matter how hard she'd tried to control it.

Mrs. Throgmorton was staring at her husband closely. "Why would he get a treat in the morning?" she asked slowly. "He never gets his treat until the afternoon, once I've picked him up. It's his reward for having to be away from me."

"I just got it mixed up is all!" Mr. Throgmorton protested.

"I do find it interesting," Courtney continued, starting to see more clues pop out as she thought about it, "that you never referred to Sir Glitter by his name. It was always 'that dog' or 'her dog.' And in the same magazine where I saw the article about him winning a show, he was also endorsing a doggie insurance policy."

Mrs. Throgmorton's face was inches from her husband's as she scowled at him. "You never did like him."

"No, I didn't!" Mr. Throgmorton burst out, causing everyone in the room to take a step back. "He's been an absolute pain in the neck ever since you brought him home! You said you needed a companion while I was away on business trips. That was fine. But I'm retired now, and still you spend every single second with that dog!"

"Wait. Hold on." Martin stepped forward, spreading his hands. "Are you telling me that the very people who hired me were also the criminals? Oh, this isn't going to look good on my resume."

"Nobody looks at it anyway, Mack," Detective Fletcher commented.

"Only one of them," Mrs. Throgmorton snarled. "Now what did you do with my baby! Tell me where he is!"

Her husband sighed, utterly exhausted. "I went in, made sure Dora wasn't looking, and took him out of the cage. I snuck him out the back door to a buddy of mine, who was going to hold onto him until we could find a suitable buyer. I didn't even think about the insurance policy."

Courtney's shoulders sagged in relief. At least that meant the dog was still alive. There were lots of down sides to everything that'd happened, but at least the dog hadn't been killed.

"You horrible, horrible man!" Mrs. Throgmorton snatched the nearest thing at hand, which happened to be a bag of gourmet dog treats the hotel had for sale. She smacked him across the arm with it. "How dare you take my baby away from me? If there's a single hair on his precious little head that's been harmed, I'm taking it out on you!" She smacked him several more times, building in intensity.

"All right, that's enough." Detective Fletcher took her by the arm and pulled her gently back. "Sir, you'll need to come with me."

Mr. Throgmorton had flinched against his wife's assault, but he blanched as white as a cloud at the idea of going to the station. "Can't I just call my attorney?"

"You can do that when we get downtown," Fletcher replied wearily. "That's how it works."

"And you'd better not call *my* attorney," Mrs. Throgmorton declared. "Actually, I'm going to go call him right now and get him on retainer. Detective Fletcher, when will I have my baby back?"

The big man lifted a hand and gestured at his new detainee. "I just need him to give me the address, and then we'll get it done."

"Tell him!" She stepped forward and smacked her husband with the dog treats once again. "Tell him right now!" *Smack, smack, smack, smack!* The trio headed out into the parking lot, with Martin Duffy on their tail. The little man waved his hands as he followed them

"That was certainly unusual," Ms. O'Donnell commented. "At least that drama is over with."

"Yes," Courtney agreed, "but there's still something else we need to address. When I took this job, I assumed I would get some training. I honestly don't know what I'm doing here. I don't know how to place supply orders or do payroll or anything else. It's not that I can't figure it out, I'm sure, but I don't know how you guys like to do things here."

Ms. O'Donnell's face reddened, and she glanced from side to side to make sure Dora and Jessi had gone back to their work. "Can I make a confession?"

"It seems to be a good day for it," Courtney cracked.

"I don't really know what your job is, either," she admitted. "I started the rescue simply because I wanted to help the animals, and I started the hotel because I knew we needed money, but I don't really have a good head for business. The last manager I had always just did whatever she wanted. Since it seemed to be going well enough, I never questioned it. I'm sorry."

"That's okay," Courtney replied genuinely. "I guess we'll just figure it out together."

CHAPTER TEN

"Courtney, did you see that we have some new volunteers coming in next week?" Jessi asked as the two of them coordinated giving the dog kennels on the rescue side a deep cleaning. It was something Courtney had noticed needed to be done, and so they'd made time for it. So far, it was turning out that managing this place had less to do with knowing the perfect schedule and more to do with tackling whatever popped up. It wasn't as planned and organized as her work in marketing, but it was a whole different animal.

"I didn't, but that's great! I was thinking we needed to get into a better bathing routine with these guys, and maybe even some of the cats. People will be more likely to adopt them if they smell better."

Jessi laughed. "Then our new volunteers can be in charge of that, especially when it comes to the cats. Mr. Throgmorton and his friend who helped steal Sir Glitter have been sentenced to community service, and they have to do it here in order to benefit the animal community. I'm always trying to get more volunteers, and at least now we'll get forty hours apiece out of them."

"I assume they'll have to stay on the rescue side?" Sir Glitter was once again coming in for regular appointments, and Courtney highly doubted his owner would want him to be anywhere near the culprits.

"Yes, definitely. But I'll be sending them out on walks with the dogs, and they can clean the cat litter. I wonder if I can get away with having them sod the yard so we can get some better grass in the play area." Jessi grinned as she squeegeed out a kennel and moved to the next one.

"Maybe. I figure we should use them as much as possible, though. This place is busy enough for a few more people to pitch in." In fact, as Courtney had started to settle into her new job, she was thinking about bringing that point up to Ms. O'Donnell. The Curly Bay Pet Hotel and Shelter could run decently with just the four of them, especially once Courtney got the owner up to speed on managing some of the paperwork, but if they had any sort of emergency or someone was sick, those pets would be out of luck.

"Are you starting to feel a little more comfortable here?" Jessi asked, looking at Courtney with genuine concern. "I'm sorry if Dora or I did anything to make you feel like we didn't want you. It's just that we're always so busy, and it makes things a lot more stressful to have to train someone on top of our regular duties."

Courtney smiled. "I completely understand. And yes. Things are going pretty well. Ms. O'Donnell and I are learning side-by-side. We even figured out the payroll, so you'll be sure to get your check next week. I admit I wasn't confident at first, but I think it's all going to work out."

Jessi nodded. "I felt pretty overwhelmed when I started here. There were so many cats and dogs that needed my help. I want to help all of them, and I want them to get everything they deserve and more. I've had to accept the fact that I can only do my best, but I think at the end of the day these guys are still pretty grateful. Isn't that right, Roger?" She ruffled the ears of a big hound.

The bell over the front door dinged. "I'll get that," Courtney said, striding into the foyer.

Mrs. Throgmorton was waiting patiently for her with Sir Glitter in his arms. He seemed none the worse for wear from his kidnapping. In fact, he looked just as fancy and pampered as always with his little sailor suit on. "Good morning, dear," she enthused. "Sir Glitter is here for his nail appointment."

Courtney had already looked over the schedule for the day, so she didn't need to fuddle with the computer system. "Not a problem! I'll take him right back, and he should be ready in an hour or so. Did you need anything special added on? Nail polish? Buffing?"

"Just the usual is fine," Mrs. Throgmorton said with a nod.

"I did see that he's due for his kennel cough shot, so if you could just get proof of that from his vet in the next week or two that'd be great." Courtney smiled, knowing a request like this could be the true test of the tentative relationship the two of them were building.

"Not a problem." Mrs. Throgmorton turned to leave, but then she turned back and tapped her fingers on the counter. "I want to apologize to you."

"There's no need."

"Yes, there is," her client insisted. "I was truly terrible to you. I accused you of stealing Sir Glitter simply because I was scared, and you seemed like someone I could point the finger at. I asked that awful private investigator to follow you around. He's not the greatest, I know, but I was desperate. And when you came to my house to try to work things out like adults, I just threw flowers in your face. I'm very ashamed of the way I acted."

Courtney had been thinking about the woman's behavior quite a bit, actually. "I understand. I didn't appreciate it at the time, but I know now you were simply scared and upset about losing someone who was so important to you. Anyone else might've done something similar."

Mrs. Throgmorton frowned. "Maybe, but this whole incident has made me realize that I've been awful to people for a long time. I don't have an excuse for that, but I'm going to work on it. And I'd also like to make up to you for what I've done. I want to do that in the best way I know how."

"What's that?" Courtney shifted Sir Glitter's minute weight in her arms, and the dog reached up to lick her chin.

"Money. I can't deny that I'm a wealthy woman, and I should use that to the best of my abilities. I'm going to organize a big fundraiser for this place. I'll invite all my friends who move in the right circles, as well. There's only one problem." She twisted her rings on her fingers.

This conversation was just getting more and more interesting. "I'm sure we can handle it."

"I have all the money and connections, but I don't know much about doing fundraisers. I don't know how to organize something that reaches out into the community like that and really gets in touch with people."

Courtney grinned. "I can't say I'm a party planner, but I've got some skills that just might help us with that. How about the two of us get together for lunch sometime this week and talk about it?"

"It's a date," Mrs. Throgmorton said with a smile.

Courtney called her mom that night. "Hi, Mom."

"Oh, honey! You sound wonderful!"

She felt wonderful, especially compared to everything she'd gone through that first week in Curly Bay. "How do you know?"

"I'm your mother, and I can hear it in your voice." Knitting needles clacked together in the background. "Are things all wrapped up with the case?"

"They are." Courtney gave her a quick rundown, including Mrs. Throgmorton's offer of a fundraiser.

"You certainly can't say that things are boring outside the city," her mother cracked. "You've had more adventure and excitement in Curly Bay than you ever did before!"

Courtney leaned back against the couch cushions, smiling up at the ceiling. What she'd thought was exciting in the city amounted to going out for dinner with Sam. Here, she was actually doing some good in the world. It hadn't been fun to worry about going to jail, but she was definitely happy here. "You're absolutely right, Mom."

THANK YOU FOR CHOOSING A PUREREAD BOOK!

We hope you enjoyed the story, and as a way to thank you for choosing PureRead we'd like to send you this free Special Edition Cozy, and other fun reader rewards…

Click Here to download your free Cozy Mystery
PureRead.com/cozy

Thanks again for reading.
See you soon!

OTHER BOOKS IN THIS SERIES

The Missing Pom Mystery

The Case of the Confused Canine

A Case Full of Cats

A Furry case of Foul Play

The Case of a Beagle and a Body

A Case of Canines, Cats, & Costumes

A Case of Frauds and Friendly Lizards

A Very Furry Christmas Mystery

The Mysterious Case of Books, Barks, & Burglary

Also, be sure to get your free copy of Sunny Cove Sleuths

PureRead.com/cozy

OUR GIFT TO YOU

AS A WAY TO SAY THANK YOU WE WOULD LOVE TO SEND YOU THIS SPECIAL EDITION COZY MYSTERY FREE OF CHARGE.

Our Reader List is 100% FREE

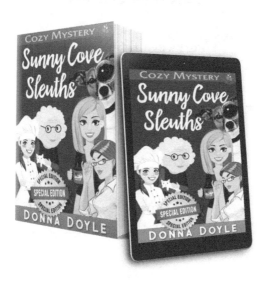

Click Here to download your free Cozy Mystery
PureRead.com/cozy

At PureRead we publish books you can trust. Great tales without smut or swearing, but with all of the mystery and romance you expect from a great story.

Be the first to know when we release new books, take part in our fun competitions, and get surprise free books in your inbox by signing up to our Reader list.

As a thank you you'll receive this exclusive Special Edition Cozy available only to our subscribers...

Click Here to download your free Cozy Mystery
PureRead.com/cozy

Thanks again for reading.
See you soon!

Made in United States
Cleveland, OH
29 July 2025